D0489288

Books should be returned or renewed by the last date above. Renew by phone **03000 41 31 31** or online *www.kent.gov.uk/libs*

Libraries Registration & Archives

ERIC
and the
GREEN-EYED GOD

Collect them all!

Eric and the Striped Horror
Eric and the Wishing Stone
Eric and the Pimple Potion
Eric and the Green-Eyed God
Eric and the Voice of Doom
Eric and the Peculiar Pong

No. 1 Boy Detective series:

The Disappearing Daughter
The Popstar's Wedding
How To Be a Detective
Spycatcher
Serious Graffiti
Dog Snatchers
Under Cover
Gruesome Ghosts
Football Forgery
The Mega Quiz

For older readers:

Billy's Blitz
Dangerous Diamonds
Run Rabbit Run
Secret Suffragette
Storm Runners
A Twist of Fortune

ERIC
and the
GREEN-EYED GOD

BARBARA MITCHELHILL
Illustrated by Tony Ross

Andersen Press
LONDON

For the children of Priorslee School who knew Eric from the beginning

This edition published in Great Britain in 2020 by
Andersen Press Limited
20 Vauxhall Bridge Road
London SW1V 2SA
www.andersenpress.co.uk

First published in 2001 by Andersen Press Limited

2 4 6 8 10 9 7 5 3 1

British Library Cataloguing in Publication Data available.

ISBN 978 1 78344 901 9

Printed and bound in Great Britain
by Clays Limited, Elcograf S.p.A.

ONE

When Eric woke up, he knew that something terrible was going to happen. He could feel it in his bones. It wasn't just that Mum was getting married on Saturday. Or that she was marrying his teacher. That was bad enough. (To be honest it was *really embarrassing!*) But he'd got used to it – sort of.

No! The real problem was this – Eric's crazy, trekking-around-the-world Auntie Rose was coming to the wedding. Doom! Auntie Rose spelled T.R.O.U.B.L.E. The presents she sent from South America had already turned Eric's world upside down.

So, if her presents could do that – what could Auntie Rose herself do? He dreaded to think! He tried pushing it to the back of his mind. But he couldn't. Saturday's wedding loomed like a black cloud on the horizon.

Somehow, Eric dragged himself out of bed and went downstairs. Mum was in the kitchen singing a soppy song about love. Eric felt worse than ever.

'You look half-asleep, duck,' she said, handing him a slice of toast. 'Have some breakfast.' She hardly paused before she burst into song again, unaware of Eric's misery.

He reached for the marmalade and spread an extra-thick layer on the toast, just to cheer himself up. As he took the first bite, he noticed a letter on the worktop. The handwriting was bold and black and familiar.

'Is that from Auntie Rose?' he said, pointing at the envelope.

Mum stopped singing.

'Yes, duck,' she said. 'And I'm afraid it's bad news.'

Eric paused mid-chew, his cheeks bulging with soggy bread and marmalade.

'Sorry, love,' she said with a deep sigh. 'Rose isn't coming to the wedding. She can't make it.'

Eric could hardly believe his luck. This was good news of double mega proportions! He wanted to leap off his chair. Jump round the room. Fling open the window and tell the world. He felt great! No Auntie Rose. No presents. No magic.

But the feel-good factor didn't last long. In fact, it only lasted until Mum went upstairs and Eric read the letter.

Dear Christine,

I'm having terrible trouble getting a flight home. The floods caused havoc at the airport. So I'll miss your wedding. Boohoo! Please send me some photographs. I'm dying to see the dress.

I'm thinking of moving down to Ecuador next – or maybe Peru. I know I said I'd only stay another month or so, but I love South America! It's really exciting!

I've been staying with a family with twelve children and they are all so friendly. They said I should send you this local fertility symbol as a wedding present. Every bride in these parts is given one. People tell me it has magic powers. Tee-hee! So, watch out, Christine! You never know.

Anyway, magic powers or not, it's made of real gold and the stones are emeralds! I hope you like it. I think it's beautiful.

With love and kisses. Have a wonderful day.

From Rose
P.S. Hello Eric! XX

Eric shivered as he read the words 'magic powers'. Auntie Rose thought it was a joke. But it was no joke!

Everything she had sent so far had caused chaos. It was because of her that Mum and The Bodge (his teacher) went all soppy over each other and decided to get married. They even KISSED sometimes. Yuck! How could they at their age?

He read the letter again. Auntie Rose had sent a 'fertility symbol'. He had to find out what it was because he had to stay clear of it.

He went to the bottom of the stairs. 'Mum!' he shouted. 'What present did Auntie Rose send you?'

There was a pause, then Mum called back. 'It's a surprise! You'll see it on Saturday. Now get a move on, Eric, or you'll be late for school.'

Eric grunted and went to fetch his bag. He couldn't help wondering what a fertility symbol looked like. He hadn't a clue. He decided to ask his best friend, Wesley.

TWO

'A fertility symbol?' said Wesley, as they walked towards the school gate. 'Dunno, Ez. Unless it's one of those brass things drummers hit on a drum kit.'

'Don't think so, Wez,' said Eric glumly. 'Not that kind of cymbal.'

Wez sighed. 'Then I've never heard of one.'

Eric was worried. If he didn't know what a fertility symbol looked like . . . how could he avoid it?

The whistle blew in the playground and everyone began to file indoors.

'I've got to find out,' said Eric, moving slowly across the tarmac.

'We could look it up,' said Wez. 'There are some big dictionaries in the library. They've got hard words in them.'

Eric grinned. 'Smart thinking, Wez. We'll go after dinner.'

That morning in assembly, Mrs Cracker (known as the Big Cheese) announced a new project.

'As your head teacher,' she said, 'I am very concerned about conservation and recycling. So, when the mayor suggested we take part in a project called "Loving the Earth", I thought it was an excellent idea.'

There was a general buzz around the hall.

The Big Cheese continued. 'The whole school will join in,' she said, 'and you will all be Pollution Detectives.'

8

Everyone looked blank. Heads turned. Hands shot up. One or two called, 'Miss?' They were puzzled.

But the head teacher waved her hand. 'I'll explain,' she said. 'Each class will look out for litter or pollution that can be poisonous to wildlife. Think of the ways of making our world a nicer place. Think of ways of recycling.'

There were groans all round. It didn't sound like much fun.

'There will be a prize for the best class presentation,' she said. 'And this will be donated by the mayor himself.'

That made all the difference. The mayor was very rich and well known for his fabulous prizes. Last year he paid for a bunch of kids to go on holiday.

'Right,' said The Bodge, when they returned to class. 'Who's got an idea?'

'Me!' called out Brent Dwyer, the class bully. 'I've got a brilliant camera. I'll go round following people like they do on TV. *Spot the Litter Lout.*'

The Bodge frowned. 'Following people could get you into trouble, Brent,' he said. 'But you could write a diary. Keep a lookout around school and around town. Maybe take your own photographs of litter or pollution.'

Wez put his hand up. 'How about a noticeboard with a picture of the "Polluter of the Week"?'

Everybody thought it was a great idea. And Wez blinked with pleasure.

'Before we start,' said The Bodge, 'we need to choose a Chief Pollution Detective.'

'What's one of those, sir?' someone asked.

'The Chief will control the project,' he explained, 'and will present it to the mayor.'

Brent Dwyer leaped up and down, desperate to be chosen. But The Bodge had other ideas.

'I want you all to write the name of the person you want to be the project leader,' he said, giving out pieces of paper. 'The one who gets the most votes will be the Chief.'

Brent Dwyer grabbed hold of some of the smaller kids.

'Vote for me or I'll thump yer,' he hissed.

It didn't work except for Calvin Thomas, who wrote Brent's name on his piece of paper. But when Brent's back was turned, Eric saw Calvin screw it up and drop it in the bin.

After the break, The Bodge announced the results.

Eric got the most votes. This was mainly because he had scored three goals in the match against Welling Road School the previous afternoon. All the team had voted for Eric. Wez had also voted for Eric. And *Eric* had voted for Eric. No contest!

As the Bodge pinned a large round badge on his chest, everyone cheered. Except for Brent Dwyer, who had plans for Eric's downfall.

THREE

At dinnertime, Eric and Wez went to the library to look for the dictionaries.

There were two large books with navy covers. One was marked *A-M*. The other was marked *N-Z*.

Eric lifted *A-M* off the shelf and slapped it on a table.

He soon found the word 'fertility' and read it out loud. 'It means *fruitfulness and productiveness*. Better write it down, eh?'

Wez pulled out his notebook and wrote what Eric had said (although the spelling wasn't exactly the same).

They heaved the dictionary back on the shelf and took the other one down.

'Symbol,' Eric said proudly and found the right page. 'It means *mark, token, ticket or watchword*.'

'Got it, Ez.'

When Wez had finished writing, Eric looked down at the notebook. 'OK,' he said, pointing to the words. 'The fertility symbol could be a fruitfulness mark or a productiveness token.'

'Or,' said Wez, 'a productiveness ticket or a fruitfulness watchword.'

They looked at each other blankly.

'I haven't a clue what one of those looks like!' said Eric. 'These dictionaries are rubbish!'

Unluckily for them, their conversation was overheard by Annie Barnstable, THE WORST GIRL ON EARTH.

'Are you looking up rude words, Eric Braithwaite?' she said.

Eric slapped the dictionary shut and spun round.

'Trust you to think that,' he said. 'We're looking up the word "fertility symbol", if you must know. My mother's been given one for a present.'

Annie's mouth dropped open and her

eyes widened. 'A *fertility* symbol?' she said.

'Yes!' snapped Eric. 'So?'

Annie started to giggle. 'Don't you know what that is?'

'Would we need a dictionary if we did?' he replied sharply.

'Well, I know,' she said.

'So what is it?'

'It's a *special* kind of lucky charm,' she tittered.

'What do you mean "special"?'

Annie clapped her hand over her mouth.

Now she was shaking with laughter. 'It's for when people want babies!'

The colour drained from Eric's face. He was stunned.

'Babies? You mean *new* babies?'

'What else, stupid?' snapped Annie. 'And I know for a fact that fertility symbols work because my auntie had one and she had SIX babies.'

Eric's head began to spin. He felt hot then cold. He was gasping for air. Surely his mother was much too old to have babies! Never in his worst nightmares could he imagine it. But Auntie Rose's magic had always worked before. Unless he got rid of the fertility symbol, the house would soon be crammed with high chairs and nappies.

FOUR

Wez came back to Eric's house to help him look for Auntie Rose's present.

'It has to be in the spare bedroom,' said Eric, as he unlocked the back door.

'Why?' asked Wez.

'Because all the presents are up there. That's why. They're going to open them at the wedding reception.'

They dropped their coats on the floor and headed towards the stairs.

'What about your mum?'

'She's gone with The Bodge to check on the food for Saturday,' said Eric. 'We've got plenty of time. Come on!'

They went straight to the smallest bedroom which was full of boxes wrapped in fancy paper with ribbons and bows.

There were masses of them.

'How do we find the fertility symbol, Ez?'

Eric gave a deep sigh. 'Just look at the label on the presents,' he said.

'Yeah,' said Wez. 'But what does it *look* like?'

'It's made of gold with emeralds stuck in it. Auntie Rose said so in her letter,' Eric explained. 'We'll know it when we see it.'

There were a surprising number of presents without labels and some had such shocking writing that they were illegible. The boys began to unwrap the parcels one by one. There were three glass vases, a china tea set, a red kettle, a green necklace and several silver photo frames. But, so far, there was nothing made of gold.

Before long, the room was in a terrible mess. The floor was covered in opened boxes and screwed-up wrapping paper.

'Shouldn't we clear up?' said Wez. 'Your mum'll go mad if she sees all this stuff.'

Eric shook his head. 'First things first, Wez,' he said. 'Find Auntie Rose's present, then we'll tidy up.'

They had no luck until Wez opened a small square package. As he looked inside, he saw a model of a cat with pointed ears. It was made of gold and had two emerald eyes.

'WOW!' he said and held it up.

'THAT'S IT!' Eric yelled, grabbing it out of Wesley's hands. 'That's what a fertility symbol looks like, Wez! It must be some kind of South American god. Brilliant!'

'Right!' said Wez. 'A green-eyed god. Spooky! So what do we do now?'

Eric knew exactly what to do. 'We'll bury it in the back garden. Keep its power underground.'

'Shall we tidy up first?' said Wez, who really was very worried about the mess.

'Good thinking,' said Eric. 'We don't want Mum guessing what we've been up to.'

They started putting the presents back into boxes – but it wasn't easy. For a start, the tea set wouldn't fit. When Eric jammed some of the cups inside, there was a loud crunching noise.

'That sounds bad,' said Wez.

Eric shrugged as he tipped out the broken remains of three cups. 'I'll get rid of 'em,' he said. 'Mum won't notice. Anyway, we always use mugs.'

Next they tried putting back the fancy paper. But they didn't have much experience at wrapping presents. No matter how much sticky tape they used, the paper wasn't big enough to cover the boxes again. 'It must have shrunk,' said Eric. 'Typical!'

They were about to stick two pieces of paper together and try again, when they heard The Bodge's car pull up in the street.

'They're back!' said Eric, grabbing the gold cat. 'I'll hide this under my bed and bury it tomorrow. Come on! Let's get downstairs before they come in!'

In the hurry to scramble out of the bedroom, they collided. Wez reeled backwards, his arms flailing in the air.

Suddenly a huge vase toppled off the chest of drawers and went crashing to the floor, sending broken glass everywhere.

'Leave it!' hissed Eric. 'I'll see to it later.'

Within seconds, they had shot downstairs and flung themselves on the sofa. And by the time Mum and The Bodge had walked into the living room, the boys were both staring intently at the telly. They looked as if they'd been there for hours.

FIVE

After tea, when Wez had gone home, Eric said, 'I'm going to bed, Mum. I've got a terrible headache.'

'Right, duck,' Mum called over her shoulder. She didn't even look at him. She was too busy talking to The Bodge about *The Wedding*.

I could get seriously depressed, thought Eric as he plodded upstairs. *I might as well be invisible in this house.*

He went to the spare room to tidy up. But he wasn't brilliant at that sort of thing and his first mistake was in picking up the glass.

'YIKES!' he yelled as a large sliver cut into his fingers. Blood oozed from the wound and Eric let out a moan.

He was in terrible pain. In fact, he was in agony! He hopped around the room, sucking his finger and howling like a wolf.

'Eric? What's going on?' Mum called from the bottom of the stairs.

He froze on the spot. If she came up, she'd see the mess and he'd be in serious trouble. He had to do something.

He slipped across the landing into his own bedroom.

'I'm OK, Mum,' he called down weakly. 'I just banged my toe.'

That did the trick and Mum went away.

But Eric realised it was going to be hard to clear the spare room. It was directly over the living room and every noise would be heard down below.

Maybe I should wait until Mum's asleep, he thought.

So he changed into his pyjamas, found this week's comic and climbed into bed. Before he had time to turn to his favourite page, he suddenly remembered that the Green-eyed God was under his bed.

He sat up in panic. He didn't trust anything that came from Auntie Rose or from South America! He remembered the pimple potion and the wishing stone only too well.

'I'm not sleeping with that thing in my room!' he said. 'No way!'

He flung back the duvet, leaped out of bed and reached for the golden cat. Once it was wrapped in some of last year's comics, he shoved it in an old sports bag. Then, using a belt looped through the straps, he swung the bag out of the window and tied it to the drainpipe. There it hung in the steadily falling drizzle.

Eric felt safe. He went back to bed and fell into a deep, deep sleep.

SIX

The next morning, Eric overslept and was almost late for school. He just made it through the gate as the bell went.

Wez was waiting. 'Did you bury the gold cat, Ez?' he asked as they walked across the playground.

Eric shook his head. 'I couldn't with Mum around. So I brought it with me,' he said, holding out the sports bag. 'We can bury it somewhere in the flowerbeds when nobody's looking.'

They decided to do it at lunchtime. But that morning, the gardeners from the council came to cut the grass, mark out the pitches and tidy up the shrubs. They were everywhere.

Eric and Wez slipped round the back of

the bike shed where they thought they were out of sight. They squeezed behind some large shrubs and started to dig.

Before they had made much of a hole, a voice yelled, 'Hey! Don't mess around in those flowerbeds.' It was one of the workmen and he was much too big to argue with.

They slunk away. 'We'll never get rid of the Green-eyed God at this rate,' grumbled Eric.

'Wait till after school, Ez.'

Eric agreed.

That afternoon, the class made posters for the Loving the Earth project. Eric was painting a boy (who looked very much like himself) pointing at a large rubbish tip and frowning. The words read: *DON'T POLLUTE THE PLANET, OR ELSE!*

Before they had finished their work, the classroom door opened and Mrs Cracker peeped in.

'Mr Hodgetts,' she called nervously to The Bodge. 'Could I have a word, please? I'm afraid something rather unpleasant has happened.'

Everyone in the class looked up, ears wagging, and listened in to what Mrs Cracker had to say.

'I'm afraid,' she said with a tremor in her voice, 'that Mrs Braithwaite's house has been broken into. All your wedding presents have been ransacked!'

The Bodge looked horrified.

'Some have been *smashed*,' Mrs Cracker continued, 'and something has been stolen. It's dreadful! Dreadful! The police are on their way. You must go, of course. I'll look after your class.'

The Bodge left at once while Eric's cheeks began to burn. He remembered the mess he had left in the spare room. Oooops!

Wez leaned over. 'Didn't you clear up, Ez?' he whispered furtively out of the corner of his mouth.

'No,' hissed Eric. 'I was going to do it in the middle of the night but . . .'

'. . . you fell asleep, didn't you, Ez?'

Eric nodded.

'So, what are you going to do? The cops will be looking for the Green-eyed God. It's gold! It's dead valuable! You'd better take it back.'

Eric frowned. 'You don't understand, Wez! If I take it back, Mum'll have loads of babies. It's crazy!' He wiped his hand across his forehead, leaving a trail of purple paint.

'But if you don't,' said Wez, 'they'll track you down. You could end up in prison.'

'They wouldn't find it, would they?'

'Don't you ever watch cop shows?' said Wez. 'They'll get a really brilliant detective. He'll find the Green-eyed God even if we bury it in the school grounds.'

'So?'

'Your fingerprints will be all over it . . . or he'll use DNA tests – they always do.'

Their conversation was interrupted when the Big Cheese clapped her hands. 'Quiet, everyone!' she said. 'Please carry on with your work. Mr Hodgetts has had to go out and so I shall stay here until home time.'

Eric did his best to continue with his painting. But his heart wasn't in it.

'Don't worry, Ez,' Wez whispered. 'I've got a brilliant plan.'

'What?'

'We'll throw the Green-eyed God in the reservoir. It's really deep. Nobody will find it there and you won't have to go to prison. And in all that water, I bet it'll lose its magic powers.'

Eric grinned. 'Wez!' he said. 'You're a genius.'

SEVEN

When school finished for the day, Eric and Wez headed for the reservoir, as they had planned. They ran most of the way and soon reached the wire fence which surrounded it. Ignoring the warning signs that read *DANGER – KEEP OUT*, they scrambled over and jumped down onto the bank.

Eric stood and looked across the water. 'Perfect!' he said. 'I'm going to sling the bag right out into the middle.'

Wez watched in admiration as Eric whizzed it round his head like a shotputter at the Olympic Games. Round and round he whirled until he suddenly let go of the handles. Then the sports bag flew up into the air, high over the reservoir, eventually falling and landing with a great *SPLASH!*

'On target!' yelled Wez. 'Bang on target, Ez!' They jumped around cheering and slapping hands. It was a brilliant throw!

Now Eric was well rid of the Green-eyed God. It would rot in the mud and never be seen again.

But they hadn't noticed that someone had followed them.

'HEY, BRAITHWAITE!'

Eric spun round. To his horror, he saw Brent Dwyer standing at the fence.

'I saw you two behind the bike shed and I knew you were up to something,' he shouted.

'Snooping, were you?'

'Yeah,' said Brent. 'And I want to know what you dumped in the reservoir.'

'None of your business, Dwyer,' said Eric.

'We'll see about that! The Bodge will want to hear about this. You've broken into a forbidden area, you have! Polluting the reservoir! Poisoning drinking water!'

Eric pretended to ignore him.

'See that sign over there?' Brent continued. 'It says, "No dumping. Fine or imprisonment if convicted."'

'So?' Eric yelled.

Brent Dwyer came forward with his arms folded.

'Chief Pollution Detective, aren't you? I can report you to the authorities. And it'll make a great story in *The Echo*, won't it? *TEACHER'S STEPSON IN POLLUTION SCANDAL.*'

Eric felt his heart banging against his ribs. He hadn't thought about that.

Wez piped up. 'It's your word against ours.'

'No it's not,' said Brent, pointing towards the water. 'Anybody can see what you've done.'

Eric looked over his shoulder and saw that instead of staying at the bottom, the sports bag had risen back to the surface. It was bobbing about like a rubber dinghy.

Eric was speechless.

'Course,' said Brent, his beady eyes glinting. 'I might not tell 'em who ditched the bag if we come to some kind of . . . *er* . . . arrangement.'

'What sort of arrangement?'

'Bring some dosh to school tomorrow,' he said, 'and I might keep my mouth shut.'

Eric's heart sank. This was blackmail! But what could he do? He'd be in serious trouble if anyone found that he – the leader of the Loving the Earth competition – had polluted the reservoir.

There was no way out. He had to agree.

'Just out of interest,' said Brent before he left, 'what's in that bag?'

'Get lost, Dwyer,' Eric yelled. 'None of your business!'

Wez joined in. 'Yeah! Just keep your nose out.'

Brent Dwyer flapped his hand and grinned.

'Oooh! Don't lose your rag!' he said. 'But I bet it's something you want to hide, eh?' And he walked away, laughing to himself.

EIGHT

On Friday morning, Eric met Brent Dwyer behind the bike shed.

'Is that all you've got, Braithwaite?' said Brent, glowering at the miserable collection of coins in Eric's hand.

'Yeah,' said Eric. 'I haven't got no more.' (Grammar was not one of his strong points.)

The bully reached out and took the money. 'Then you'd better look out,' he sneered. 'Cos everybody's going to know what you've done.'

Eric felt gloomy for the rest of the day.

'Cheer up,' said Wez as they walked home. 'Even if Brent Dwyer tells, it's not exactly a major crime.'

'Oh no?' said Eric, deep in despair. 'The Bodge will go mad. Not to mention the mayor.'

Wez shrugged his shoulders. 'It could be worse, Ez,' he said. 'Somebody could fish the bag out and find the Green-eyed God. Then you'd be in DEEP TROUBLE!'

Eric stopped. His face turned white and a look of horror spread across his face. 'You don't think they would, do you?'

'Nah!' said Wez. 'Course not!'

But Eric was already picturing the scene as someone rowed out in a small boat to retrieve the bag.

'It's got my name on it,' he croaked. 'They'll take it to the police.'

He was now totally panic-stricken. 'The police will know I stole the Green-eyed God, Wez. I'm doomed.'

*

That night, Eric lay in bed, filled with black despair. His mum was really upset about the 'break-in' and now, if someone found the bag, he'd be looking at months and months locked in a prison cell.

NINE

The next morning was not a normal Saturday. Eric went downstairs, hoping Mum would cook a big breakfast. She usually did at the weekend. No chance! A hairdresser arrived even before he'd finished his cereal. So did Mum's friend, Sarah. Nobody heard Eric say, 'Any chance of some bacon and eggs?' The kitchen was too full of people with brushes and rollers and dryers and hairspray. It was awful!

Eric decided to disappear upstairs. He would spend the time planning his speech for that afternoon. It had to be good – he was the Best Man, after all.

Later, when he next saw Mum, she was transformed. She was wearing a long white dress and funny shoes. Her face was pink with red lips and blue stuff round her eyes.

'How do I look, Eric?' she said.

Eric played it cool. 'OK,' he said.

Mum smiled and gave him a big hug, leaving a trail of powder behind.

Eric was worried. Mum looked really different! She even *smelled* different. She was taller than before and her hair had changed colour. As for the dress – well! She usually wore jeans.

The more he thought about it, the more he realised that The Bodge might not recognise her! So, as a safety measure, he planned to point out which was Mum. He would also explain that this transformation took *hours*. She wasn't likely to do it often and she would soon be back to normal.

By twelve o'clock, Eric had washed his face and had put on a white shirt and navy blue suit and tied his tie, sort of. It was time to go and The Bodge arrived to take him to the registry office in his car. Mum, for some reason, didn't want to see him and hid on the stairs. When Eric suggested Mum and Sarah squeeze into the back of The Bodge's car, Mum refused.

It turned out she had hired a flashy black limo for the day. What a waste of money!

The Bodge and his Best Man left the house and drove into town. But when the car turned into Hamer Street, they were in for a surprise. Outside the registry office, pupils from North Street School were lined up along the drive and in the gardens at the front. It was amazing!

As The Bodge climbed out of his car, a cheer broke out. He smiled and waved and jostled his way through the crowd and into the building. Eric followed. But as he did, someone grabbed hold of his arm. It was Brent Dwyer.

'Hey, Braithwaite! Want a bag to go with your naff wedding outfit?'

When Eric turned, he saw that Brent was holding the old sports bag he had thrown into the reservoir.

Images of police and prison cells flashed before his eyes. So this was it! His life was ruined. And Brent Dwyer was the cause.

Crazy with rage, Eric lunged at the bully, who was caught off-balance and reeled backwards. All the kids gathered round at the prospect of a good fight. Eric grabbed hold of Brent's shirt. Brent grabbed hold of Eric's tie. They locked together, staggering over the grass – backwards and forwards – until they crashed into a rosebed and the sports bag dropped out of the bully's hand. Eric let go of Brent and whipped round to snatch the bag.

It was empty! He could tell by the feel of it.

'Where is it?' he yelled.

'Where's what?'

'The gold cat that was in the bag.'

'There was no cat,' Brent sneered. 'The bag was empty! I found it on the bank of the reservoir.'

'You're lying!'

'I'm not! I went back to take a photo . . .'

Eric raised his fist, ready to strike. But as he did, a big black limo drew up to the pavement and Mum stepped out.

The crowd went silent. Eric's mum stood there dressed in white lace from top to toe, wearing a shiny necklace and holding a huge bunch of flowers. But as soon as she saw the boys her face turned from pink to deep scarlet. Bursting with rage, she picked up her train and stormed across the pavement.

'JUST LOOK AT YOU!' she shouted. 'YOU OUGHT TO BE ASHAMED OF YOURSELVES. GET UP AT ONCE!'

Eric and Brent scrambled to their feet. Eric's jacket was torn and blood was streaming down his nose and dripping onto his shirt. He tried to brush soil from his suit but it only made it worse.

'What are you doing here, Brent Dwyer?' Mum demanded.

Brent looked sheepish. 'Returning Eric's bag, Mrs Braithwaite,' he said. 'I found it.'

'Huh!' said Mum. 'A likely story!'

She snatched it off him and flung it in the back of the limo.

'Now get inside the registry office, Eric!' she screeched as she pushed him ahead of her. 'You're *not* going to be late for my wedding!'

TEN

The wedding went smoothly. Thankfully nobody seemed to notice the Best Man's torn jacket or the blood on his shirt.

At the reception, Eric made a brilliant speech. Everyone laughed at the funny bits and nobody minded when he got things muddled up. When it was finished, Wez gave him the thumbs-up and mouthed the word *'Brilliant!'*

Eric winked back. He felt relaxed. He hadn't a care in the world. Even the Green-eyed God had disappeared.

He sat back as The Bodge began to make his speech. It was pretty boring, and Eric's eyelids drooped. But, just as Eric was nodding off, The Bodge said something that made him wake up and listen.

'There's one person who couldn't be here today,' said The Bodge. 'And that is Christine's sister, Rose, who is out in South America. I know we're both disappointed that she couldn't get back for the wedding.'

There were 'Oohs' and 'Ahs' around the room and cries of 'What a shame!'

Then The Bodge continued. 'But she *did* send us a very special present.'

Eric felt nervous and wondered what was coming next. Was he going to talk about the theft of the Green-eyed God? He waited to hear.

'The present,' said The Bodge, turning to Eric's mum, 'is the beautiful white gold and emerald necklace which Christine is wearing today.'

Eric's mouth fell open. He looked round at Wez, who was equally shocked. After all their trouble, they had got it wrong! The Green-eyed God was harmless! The *necklace* was the fertility symbol! He'd never heard of white gold before now. It looked like silver to him. Eric desperately needed to talk to Wez. As soon as the speeches were finished, they met up.

'It's the worst day of my life!' said Eric, as they slipped under a table for a bit of peace and quiet. 'Mum's wearing the fertility symbol. I'm doomed!'

Wez was sympathetic. He passed Eric a can of cola, a large bag of smoky bacon crisps and a plate of sausage rolls. 'Cheer up, Ez. Surely not all fertility symbols work.'

'This one will!' said Eric, dipping into the crisps. 'Our house will be full of crying babies. Hundreds of 'em. Just you see.'

'Well,' said Wez wisely. 'Look on the bright side. When it's Mum's turn to look after my baby sister, Dad likes to get out

for a bit. That's when he takes me fishing.'

As Eric slowly filled his mouth with crisps, he pondered Wez's words.

One crying baby = one day's fishing. Oh well! Maybe life wasn't so bad, after all.

ERIC
and the
STRIPED HORROR

BARBARA MITCHELHILL
Illustrated by Tony Ross

Eric is more sporty than brainy, but a big test is looming. Then his auntie sends him a very strange present: an ugly, stinky, stripy jumper with magical powers. It can turn the wearer into a genius. Will it work on him?

978 1 78344 796 1